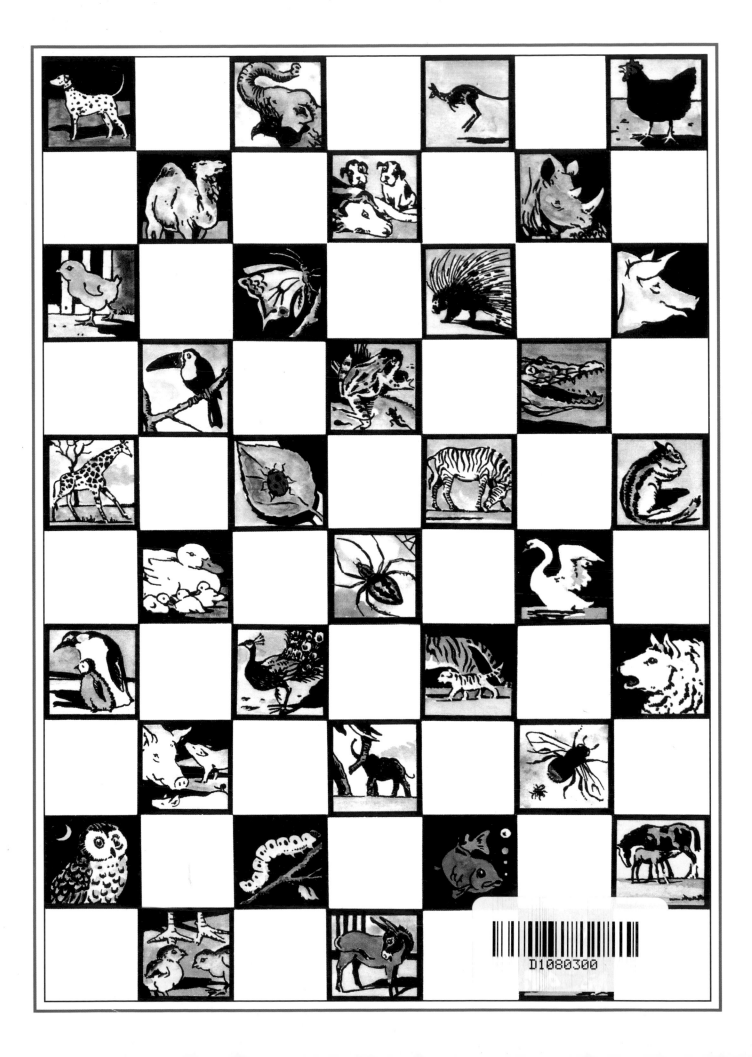

A DORLING KINDERSLEY BOOK

Illustrations by
Jonathan Heale

First published in Great Britain in 1993
by Dorling Kindersley Limited,
9 Henrietta Street, London, WC2E 8PS

Reprinted 1994, 1995

Photography (Title page penguins; page 10
orang-utan; page 12 jaguar; page 15 toucan, camel;
page 19 tiger cub; page 20 jaguar; Jacket tiger cub)
copyright © 1991 Philip Dowell
Photography (Imprint page butterfly; page 7 cockatoo, wolf;
page 9 duck; page 10 butterfly; page 12 ladybirds; page 13 fish;
page 14 rhinoceros, fox, crocodile; page 16 ladybird)
copyright © 1991 Jerry Young
Photography (page 8 polar bear) copyright © 1992 Jerry Young
Photography (Title page rabbit kittens; page 11 rabbit;
page 18 rabbit; page 19 rabbit kittens; page 20 duck)
copyright © 1991 Barrie Watts

A CIP catalogue record for this book is
available from the British Library

ISBN 0-7513- 5051-6

Colour reproduction by Colourscan
Printed in Italy by L.E.G.O.

For Rose,
Samuel, and
Florence

BABY'S BOOK OF
ANIMALS

Roger Priddy

DORLING KINDERSLEY

LONDON • NEW YORK • STUTTGART

What do I say?

kitten

Mee-ow

donkey

Ee-aw
Ee-aw

calves

Ooo
Ooo
Ooo

chimpanzee

Moooo
Moooo

6

cockatoo

Howwlll

Squark Squark

wolf

pig

hen
and
chicks

Oink Oink

Cluck
Cluck

Cheep-cheep-cheep-cheep-cheep-cheep

What we say

dog

Woof Woof

Grrowwll

Baaa

Baaa

sheep

mouse

Squeak-squeak-squeak-squeak

polar bear

8

QuackQuack

duck

WhOo WhOooo

owls

Neighhh   horse

Rrroarrr

lion

red
parrot

blue
butterfly

orange orang-utan

black panther

brown bear

white rabbit

green lizard

yellow
ducklings

Spotty animals

ladybirds

moth

giraffe

dalmatian

jaguar

Stripey animals

tigers

chipmunk

zebra

fish

Animal features

A flamingo has a long neck and long legs.

This rhinoceros has horns on its nose.

A porcupine is very prickly.

This fox has very big ears.

A crocodile has lots of sharp teeth.

14

A toucan has a big beak.

An elephant has a long trunk.

This camel has a hump.

A kangaroo has a long tail and very big back feet.

Creepy crawlies

butterfly

wasp

moth

bee

ladybird

damselfly

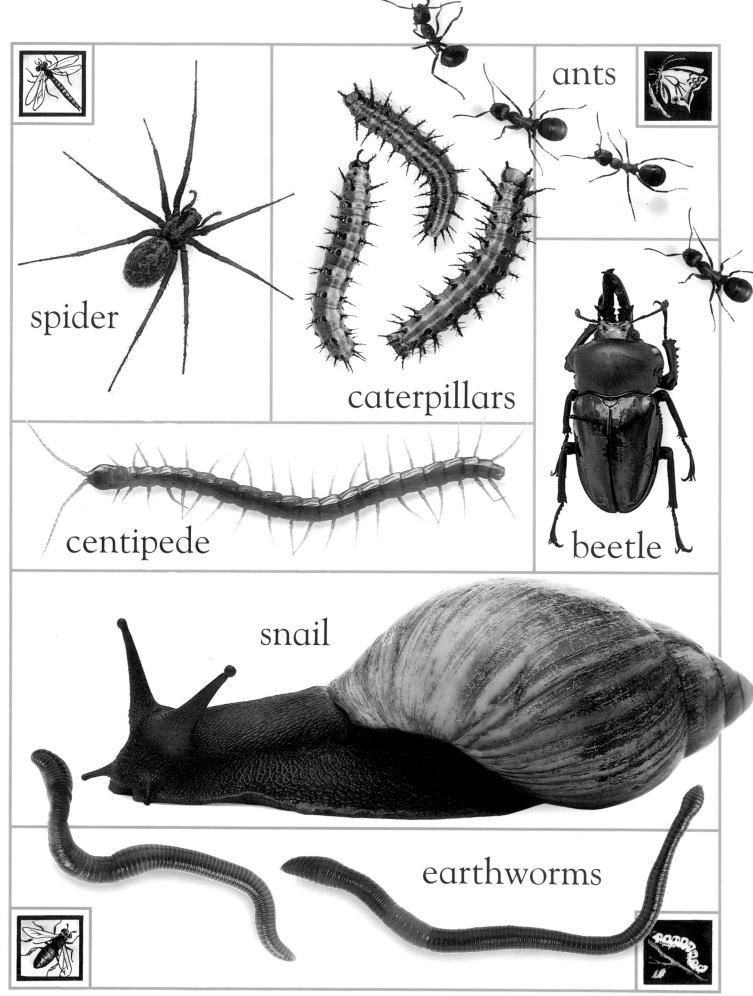

spider

caterpillars

ants

beetle

centipede

snail

earthworms

Find my baby

tiger

sheep

dog

hen

rabbit

giraffe

puppies

lamb

rabbit kittens

chicks

tiger cub

giraffe calf

19

leopard

cow

pig

zebra

cat

duck

20

kittens

piglet

duckling

leopard
cub

calf

zebra
foal